Mama's Right Here

By **Susan Kerner**
Illustrated by **Estelle Corke**

STAR BRIGHT BOOKS
Cambridge, Massachusetts

Published in the United States of America by Star Bright Books, Inc.
The name Star Bright Books and the Star Bright Books logo are registered trademarks of Star Bright Books, Inc. Please visit: www.starbrightbooks.com.
For bulk orders email: orders@starbrightbooks.com,
or call customer service at: (617) 354-1300.

Hardback ISBN-13: 978-1-59572-701-5
Star Bright Books / MA/ 00103150
Paperback ISBN-13: 978-1-59572-702-2
Star Bright Books / MA / 00103150

Printed in China (Toppan) 10 9 8 7 6 5 4 3 2 1

Printed on paper from sustainable forests and a percentage of post-consumer paper.

Library of Congress Cataloging-in-Publication Data

Kerner, Susan.
 Mama's right here / by Susan Kerner ; illustrated by Estelle Corke.
    pages cm
 Summary: A rhyming story in which a child describes all of the ways Mama's presence can be felt--in dandelion seeds that float through the air and the sound of raindrops on leaves--even though she is not there like most mothers.
 ISBN 978-1-59572-701-5 (hardback) -- ISBN 978-1-59572-702-2 (pbk.)
 [1. Stories in rhyme. 2. Mothers--Fiction. 3. Loss (Psychology)--Fiction.] I. Corke, Estelle, illustrator. II. Title.
III. Title: Mama is right here.
 PZ8.3.K3985Mam 2015
 [E]--dc23
                        2014040613

For Lily, My Love.
Ever together,
even when we're apart.

If you ask me where my mama is,
   this is what I'll say:
"She's in me and around me, never far away."

She's in the golden glow
of the afternoon sun,

In the feather-soft snow when winter's just begun,

In the dandelion seeds that float through the air,

In the delicate breeze that rustles my hair.

Daddy says that when I laugh
and crinkle up my nose,

That I'm my mother's child
from my head to my toes.

Grandma says I'm just like Mama
when I gaze up at the sky,

The way I roll in the leaves
and breathe a gentle sigh.

I can see her in the stars
   of the bright night sky.
She's the face in the moon.
I'm the apple of her eye.

And when I feel the ocean waves
nudge me toward the sand,
I know it's Mama guiding me
gently by the hand.

Sometimes I wish she could see me run
or admire my high-flying kite,

Stroke my back as I fall asleep
and kiss my cheek good-night.

But I know she's always with me
in the beating of my heart.

It's her rhythm that gets me dancing.
She's the color in my art.

It's her calming voice I hear when
the raindrops touch the leaves.

It's her strength that I admire
in the branches of the trees.

I'm told I have her smile
and her very dramatic flair.

"There's just one you," says Daddy.
"But there are traits that you two share."

"So as your sparkling life brightens up the world,
  with an all-knowing smile you'll say,
'My mama is in me and everywhere—
  she's just here in a different way.'"